DOCTOR·WHO

⬡ DECIDE YOUR DESTINY

Avoch
Primary
School

BBC CHILDREN'S BOOKS
Published by the Penguin Group
Penguin Books Ltd, 80 Strand, London, WC2R 0RL, England
Penguin Group (USA) Inc., 375 Hudson Street, New York, New York 10014, USA
Penguin Books (Australia) Ltd, 250 Camberwell Road, Camberwell, Victoria 3124, Australia.
(A division of Pearson Australia Group Pty Ltd)
Canada, India, New Zealand, South Africa
Published by BBC Children's Books, 2007
Text and design © Children's Character Books, 2007
Written by Trevor Baxendale
10 9 8 7 6 5 4 3 2 1
BBC and logo © and TM BBC 1996. Doctor Who logo © BBC 2004. TARDIS image © BBC 1963.
Dalek image © BBC/Terry Nation 1963. Licensed by BBC Worldwide Limited.
DOCTOR WHO, TARDIS and DALEK and the DOCTOR WHO, TARDIS and DALEK logos are
trade marks of the British Broadcasting Corporation and are used under licence.
ISBN-13: 978-1-40590-382-0
ISBN-10: 1-40590-382-1
Printed in Great Britain by Clays Ltd, St Ives plc

DOCTOR · WHO

DECIDE YOUR DESTINY

War of
the Robots

by Trevor Baxendale

War of the Robots

1 | On the way home from the corner shop, you literally walk right into an old blue police box. You're sure it wasn't there a moment ago. The door creaks open and a strange light shines out. Intrigued, you step inside and find yourself walking up a metal gangway into an enormous chamber.

Two people are standing at a complex central control console. One of them is a pretty young woman and she notices you immediately. She elbows the person next to her — a tall, thin man in a suit and sticky-up hair. He looks up at you with wide, enquiring eyes.

This is the Doctor and Martha. The introductions are made quickly, because the whole control room is shuddering as the central column pulsates with green light.

'This is a time and space machine called the TARDIS,' Martha explains as you hang on to the rail. 'I'm afraid we've already taken off.'

'Where are we going?' you ask, feeling anxious and thrilled at the same time.

'Absolutely no idea,' declares the Doctor, as he frantically operates the controls. 'You stepping on-board at the last moment has upset the helmic regulators. Hang on, I'll try to materialize...'

The noise and shaking eventually stop, and the Doctor and Martha head for the doors. The Doctor grabs a long brown coat on his way out, shouting for you to hurry up and join them.

The TARDIS has landed on an alien world in the distant future. The police box stands in the middle of a huge crater, looking very out of place.

The crater is filled with rubble and bits of metal — debris from the massive explosion that has blown a deep hole in the ground. In the green sky above, clouds of black smoke drift over the crater, dragging the sounds of battle with them. You can hear explosions and the crackle of gunfire in the distance.

'I don't like it here much,' says Martha, wincing as another bomb explodes — this one seems a lot nearer. 'Couldn't we go somewhere warm and sunny?'

'Hmm,' the Doctor replies, standing up. 'We've got a choice — go back to the TARDIS and try somewhere else or stay and have a look around here first... see what's going on. What d'you say?'

If you choose to go back to the TARDIS, go to 35. If you choose to stay and explore, go to 51.

2 The sky station's engines are deafening. You both cover your ears as the flyer is sucked into one of the tractor chutes beneath the craft, like grit into a vacuum cleaner.

The flyer floats to a halt and is grabbed by huge mechanical latches. There are robot guards waiting for you. They drag you off the flyer and march you through several gloomy corridors until they reach a heavy metal doorway.

'Where are you taking us?' asks Martha. 'What is this place?'

'THIS IS MACHINA 1,' the robot tells you.

The door clangs open and the robot throws you and Martha inside.

The door closes behind you. The prison cell is small and bare except for one thing — the Doctor's sitting in the corner.

'Wondered when you two would turn up,' he says, jumping to his feet. 'Welcome to Machina 1 — the HQ of the robots. Well, this particular lot of robots anyway.'

'Doctor, it's great to see you!'

'Couldn't agree more. And now that you're both here we can escape!' He whips out his sonic screwdriver with a crafty grin.

If the Doctor opens the cell door, the robot could still be outside. If you want to chance it, go to 29. Or if you think he should look for another way out, go to 91.

3 You quickly tell the Doctor about Martha, and the two of you hurry over to help.

'What was that thing?' asks Martha.

'War robot,' explains the Doctor. 'The explosion hurled me out of the crater. I've had a chance to look around and it's not good. We're in the middle of a battle between armoured robots.'

With the Doctor's help you can move the rock enough for Martha to pull her leg free. Together you lift her up between you. 'I think I can walk,' she says. 'But where's the TARDIS?'

You look around the blasted remains. There's no sign of the police box anywhere.

'We can't wait around here much longer,' says the Doctor urgently. 'We'd better — '

More armoured robots appear at the top of the crater, levelling their guns at the three of you. 'STOP WHERE YOU ARE.'

If you raise your hands to surrender, go to 47. If you make a break for it, go to 117.

4 | You look to see what the Doctor's doing. He's already running towards the fallen girl.

She's wearing military fatigues, and she appears to have crawled away from the crashed vehicle. She must be badly injured.

'Hello!' the Doctor says kindly, introducing himself. 'What's happened here, then? Taken a tumble?'

'Flyer crashed,' replies the girl through teeth clenched in pain. 'Shot down by a robot skimmer. Guess I'm lucky to be alive. What are you doing?'

'Just checking for internal injuries.' The Doctor is running his sonic screwdriver over the girl's body. He checks the reading and confers briefly with Martha, who is a medical student. She and the Doctor exchange a solemn look. It's obvious the girl's injuries are fatal.

'All clear,' Martha smiles gently. 'Cuts and contusions only.'

The girl manages a brave smile. 'I doubt it... I haven't got long and you know it.'

Go to 11.

5 | **W**ithout thinking, you run towards the girl. You hear Martha scream behind you, 'No — wait!'

But it's too late.

As you race towards the fallen girl, something bursts out of the sand in front of you. Covered in grime, a humanoid figure emerges like a corpse from a grave. But beneath the dirt you can see burnished metal and a tangle of wires and pistons. Green eyes glow in a metallic face.

It's some kind of robot.

It raises a large, heavy rifle and aims it right at your head.

'ALL HUMANS MUST DIE!' it proclaims in a harsh, steely voice.

You throw yourself to one side, and the robot opens fire. Brilliant beams of blue energy burn the earth where you stood a second before.

Then more robots emerge from the ground, all of them armed...

Go to 98.

6 | More explosions rock the area.

'Come on,' says the Doctor, pulling Martha up. 'We haven't got time to sit around here moping! Grab that robot head!'

You scoop up the rucksack and run after them, just before the entire area is shattered by a sustained barrage of heavy mortar fire.

You hurl yourselves under a rocky outcrop for shelter as earth rains down.

'Robot wars,' mutters the Doctor disapprovingly. 'Never like 'em. They never get fed up, robots. Just keep on going no matter what.'

If you think you should keep on going too, go to 57. If you think you should stay under cover, go to 24.

7 | '**I** can't leave you here like this,' you tell her.

But Martha's left leg is stuck under a heavy piece of masonry. You can see where her jeans are torn and it looks bad.

'I'll see if I can move it.' You push the rock but it's too heavy. It won't budge.

'You'll have to find something to use as a lever,' Martha tells you.

As you look around for an iron bar among the debris, a shadow falls across you. Looking up, you see a giant armoured figure towering over you. It is covered in thick, rusting metal body armour, webbed with dirty wires and tubes. A pair of glowing green eyes stares balefully at you from a dark, metallic face.

It trudges down the crater towards you as you pick up a steel bar.

'Put down your weapon,' it orders, in a voice fizzing with static.

If you drop the steel bar, go to 9. If you stand your ground, go to 16.

8 **Q**uickly, instinctively, you raise your hands. You are unarmed — surely the robot will see that?

It takes a long time for the machine to decide. You can almost hear the gears grinding inside its head, as if an old but robust computer is calculating its next course of action.

Eventually, the gun is lowered, but the robot steps forward and grabs you by the throat. You can barely draw breath. 'YOU ARE UNARMED,' it states coldly. 'YOU ARE DESIGNATED NON-COMBATANT UNTIL FURTHER NOTICE. YOU WILL BE TAKEN FOR ANALYSIS!'

Another robot marches up. You hadn't noticed it approaching in all the excitement, but you can hear the joints creaking as the thing moves. The robots look battle-hardened but the war has taken its toll: they are dented, rusting, streaked with thick black oil and grime.

'WHERE ARE THE OTHER HUMANS?' asks the robot.

If you keep quiet, go to 17. If you reply, go to 10.

9 Almost paralysed with fear, you let go of the bar. The giant mechanical figure stalks slowly towards you. Cold metal fingers close around your throat and, one handed, the robot lifts you off the ground as if you weigh nothing.

'YOU ARE A LIVING ORGANISM,' it states. Its green eyes bore into you. 'YOU MUST BE DESTROYED.'

'Wait!' you manage to gasp, kicking and struggling. 'We need help! My friend's hurt!'

The robot's head buzzes and clicks and then turns to look at Martha, who is still trapped by the fallen rock. 'ALL LIVING ORGANISMS MUST BE DESTROYED. THIS WORLD IS FOR ROBOTS ONLY.'

'You can't just kill us,' you argue desperately. Your words tumble out in a rush. 'Martha's hurt. She's trapped. We're only here by accident anyway. Just help me to free her and we can leave!'

'Come on,' Martha urges, 'big chap like you — I bet you could lift it one-handed.'

The robot does exactly that. Still carrying you in one hand, it bends down with a whine of rusting motors and heaves the masonry off Martha's leg. With a gasp of relief she's free.

Although you both appear to be prisoners.

'ARE THERE ANY OTHER HUMANS IN THE VICINITY?' asks the robot.

You look at Martha, and she shrugs. '*What about the Doctor?*' She mouths to you. Where is he?

If you call out to the Doctor for help, go to 18. If you decide to keep quiet about him, go to 17.

10 'What other humans?' you say, struggling to speak clearly. You don't want them to know about the Doctor.

'WE HAVE ALREADY APPREHENDED ONE HUMAN AND TAKEN HIM FOR ANALYSIS,' declares the robot. 'WE ARE SEARCHING FOR HIS COMPATRIOTS.'

Could they be talking about the Doctor? You daren't give them a flicker of recognition — not yet. 'Don't know what you're talking about,' you reply. The way their green eyes shine steadily at you is disconcerting.

'TAKE THIS ONE FOR ANALYSIS,' orders the lead robot.

You are dragged over the next rise and taken to a holding post — and the Doctor. He's been handcuffed to the post but he seems otherwise unharmed. He's guarded by two more robots.

'Wondered when you'd turn up,' he smiles. 'And before you ask, I don't have a clue where Martha is.'

This is bad news, but you're relieved to find the Doctor alive and well. There's hope yet.

'I need to get these handcuffs off,' the Doctor whispers. 'D'you think you can reach my sonic screwdriver? Left-hand jacket pocket, but be careful — if these robots see you with it they'll smash it.'

If you think you can get the sonic screwdriver without being spotted, go to 40. If you think it's too risky, go to 41.

'Can we get her back to the TARDIS?' you ask.

The roar of explosives is drawing closer. You are all aware that time is running short.

'What's your name?' Martha asks the girl.

'Tela,' she says. 'I have to get back to base... make my report...'

The Doctor's eyes narrow. 'Base? Report on what?'

There's another huge explosion nearby. Tela licks her dry lips. She's clearly very weak and may not last much longer. 'The robots are making advances through the western sector. We're wide open to attack. If I can get this back to base...' She nods at a rucksack lying in the dirt next to her, 'then maybe we can work out a plan of counter-attack.'

The Doctor picks up the rucksack, which looks heavy. 'What is it?'

If you think you should look in the rucksack, go to 99. If you think there isn't enough time, go to 13.

12 The Doctor taps you on the shoulder and signals you to move. Martha is still gripping your arm so tight it feels like it's in a vice. When you look down you find that you're standing on the rat's tail.

The rat gives a loud squeak and you all freeze.

Gently you raise your foot and the rat scurries away, slipping through the water and disappearing into the darkness.

The voices have stopped.

'Come on,' whispers the Doctor. 'Let's go.'

You run silently down the tunnel towards the exit hatch. Up the metal ladder. The Doctor throws open the manhole cover and you scramble up towards the light.

Go to 73.

'No time!' you yell as another shell lands nearby. The ground shakes and debris is thrown everywhere. When you get back on your feet, Martha is holding Tela — and she looks tearful.

'Doctor! I think Tela's been hit by shrapnel!'

The Doctor scrambles over to the girl; Martha is already checking her pulse. 'I can't feel anything. I think she's dead...!'

The Doctor rests a hand on Martha's arm. 'She's gone, Martha. There's nothing we can do for her now.'

He stands up, looking serious. There's a steely determination in his eyes now — he's going to make sure Tela didn't give her life for nothing.

You pick up the remains of the rucksack, which has been ripped apart by a piece of flying shrapnel. Inside are a few electrical components in a hard metal shell, which you show to the Doctor.

'We need to get this to Tela's people,' he notes, examining the contents. 'See if it really can make a difference.'

'But how are we going to find them?' asks Martha.

If you volunteer to scout ahead and look, go to 22. If you have a better idea, go to 21.

14 'It's too dangerous,' you whisper. 'There are too many robots around. We should back off.'

' *"Discretion's the better part of valour"*,' murmurs the Doctor in agreement. 'Have you ever met Will Shakespeare?'

You shake your head.

'He's lovely,' says Martha with a cheeky grin and a wink. 'Trust me.'

'I'll take your word for it,' you mutter. The three of you withdraw and soon the sound of the robot manoeuvres has diminished. It isn't long before you stumble across something half-buried in the sand: something metallic.

'What is it? Asks Martha.

'Some kind of trapdoor,' you say.

The Doctor kneels down to investigate. 'Manhole cover,' he says with enthusiasm. 'Ooh, we've just got to have a look down here!'

Go to 36.

15

It's not easy to find your bearings in the middle of a battleground, but there is one huge column of black smoke on the horizon that you can use as a landmark. Working from that, you can tell in which direction the TARDIS landed.

You march across the desert. A merciless sun burns down from a vast green sky.

The land begins to slope upward and the going gets tougher. You plough on, and as you reach the top of the hill, you feel a sudden surge of hope.

Among the rocks below you can see the Doctor and Martha, but they are held captive by a group of robots. There is some kind of truck with caterpillar tracks standing to one side. The Doctor and Martha have their hands up, but the robots may not know what that means. They're levelling their laser weapons at your friends, ready to fire.

'Wait!' you cry out, running down to the rocks. 'Don't shoot them!'

The robots turn their impassive green eyes towards you. The Doctor and Martha look relieved to see you, but then something else catches your attention. The TARDIS! The old police box is being loaded on to the back of the truck.

Go to 68.

16 You stand up, brandishing the metal bar. You won't go down without a fight. 'Don't come any closer,' you say, trying to sound calm. 'What do you want? Who are you?'

The figure strides towards you regardless. It raises a hand and you raise your weapon in reply. 'I'm warning you!' you shout.

The hand suddenly shoots forward as the figure's arm extends with a harsh, mechanical rattle. Massive steel fingers close around your bar and wrench it painfully from your grasp.

The figure steps forward and lifts you off the ground as if you weigh nothing.

'YOU ARE A LIVING ORGANISM,' it states. Its green eyes bore into you. 'YOU MUST BE DESTROYED.'

'Wait!' you manage to gasp, kicking and struggling. 'We need help! My friend's hurt!'

The creature's head buzzes and clicks; it seems to be thinking about what you are saying.

'HOW MANY OF YOU ARE HERE?'

If you say, 'Only me and Martha,' go to 20.
If you say, 'Me, Martha and the Doctor,' go to 19.

17 You daren't say anything about the Doctor – he could be somewhere out there, planning to rescue you! As much as you want to call for help, you keep quiet.

The robot doesn't let go of your throat. After a few more seconds you pass out.

When you wake up, you're lying on the ground. There are two robots on the far side of the crater, but they're not looking your way. Maybe they've forgotten about you! Carefully, silently, you move on to all fours, ready to crawl away. You take one last look at the crater – Martha's gone and the robots still haven't noticed you.

Then you turn and make a break for it...

Right into a troop of robots marching towards you. Behind them is some kind of vehicle with stubby wings and a flat base. There's a robot standing on it with Martha.

Go to 42.

18 The robot advances threateningly on Martha.

'STOP WHERE YOU ARE,' orders the robot, raising its free hand towards your friend as she backs away.

'Leave her alone!' you gasp. 'Doctor! Quick! Help!'

But there is no reply. No answering call; no tall, dark, skinny saviour.

Just the robot — stalking towards Martha as she backs away.

'Run!' you croak. 'Martha — turn and run for your life!'

If you think Martha would run, go to 32.
If you think she would rather stay with you, go to 42.

19 | The robot scans you with its green eyes. You can feel its mechanical brain picking through your every thought and memory and realise that it would have been pointless to lie. 'YOU ARE TELLING THE TRUTH,' it states coldly. 'YOU MUST BOTH BE ELIMINATED.'

'Hang on a mo,' calls a familiar voice from behind the robot. The Doctor is hopping down from the rim of the crater. He gives you a jaunty wave and winks at Martha. 'I hope you're not discriminating against me just because I'm not human,' he tells the robot.

'YOU WILL BE TAKEN FOR ANALYSIS,' the robot replies. 'THESE TWO WILL BE ELIMINATED.'

'Really?' The Doctor looks doubtful. 'Well, you'd better hurry up then…'

You look up, suddenly aware of the high, keening whistle of a falling bomb. You can't see anything yet but you know it's coming — and so does the Doctor!

If you dive for cover, go to 33. If you sprint out of the crater, go to 32.

20 | Something makes you keep quiet about the Doctor.

'It's just me and my friend,' you say. 'She's injured and she can't move. We need help.'

The impassive green eyes turn to look at Martha, who waves cheerily from the ground. 'Hi there,' she smiles.

At first you think she's delirious, but then the Doctor suddenly steps up behind the giant, armoured figure.

'Hello,' he says, and deftly inserts his sonic screwdriver into a junction in the robot's neck armour. 'Sorry to interrupt.' There is a loud snap of an electrical short circuit and the giant sinks slowly to its knees, the green light fading from its eyes. Internal motors whine to a halt and the thing is silent.

'I don't know,' jokes the Doctor, 'I only wander off for a minute and you two are already in trouble!'

You hear the urgent crackle of gunfire close by — you're not out of danger yet.

'Come on,' advises the Doctor. 'We need to get away from this place — and fast!'

If you decide to run, go to 34. If you stay with Martha, go to 3.

21 'Wait a sec,' you say. 'Tela couldn't have been alone...' You scan the ground around you. It's muddy and there are plenty of footprints — mostly yours, Martha's shoes and the Doctor's plimsolls. But there are others, too — the big, heavy tread of army boots.

'Look,' you say, pointing. 'Footprints!'

'Oh yes!' says the Doctor with sudden enthusiasm. 'Footprints! I like it! Nothing like a bit of good old-fashioned footprint following. It's your idea — lead on!'

Martha gives a sad little look at Tela, and then follows the Doctor behind you. You try to put the dead girl out of your mind and concentrate on the task at hand. You can't take too long about it, either: there are more explosions and the sound of gunfire seems to be getting closer.

The footprints eventually lead to some kind of heavy steel hatch set into the ground, like a manhole. There are more footprints leading away from it in many directions.

If you think you should go down the manhole, go to 36. If you think you should leave it and carry on, go to 37.

22 'It could be dangerous if we all go,' you say. 'Let me scout ahead on my own.'

You move forward — and not a moment too soon, as a huge explosion suddenly tears the ground from beneath your feet. Stunned, you climb to your feet and stagger through the smoking crater.

Martha is coughing nearby. 'What was it?'

'Some kind of mortar round, I think,' you say, although it could have been anything — even a landmine. Perhaps you've arrived in the middle of a minefield!

'I can't see the Doctor anywhere,' complains Martha.

Go to 77.

---

23 'How do you monitor the fighting from up here?' you ask.

Kelzo glides across to the large computer bank. At the touch of a control, a huge panoramic view screen opens and the planet Titanius is clearly visible. It looks like a huge grey ball, streaked with orange.

The Doctor stares sadly at the screen. 'Nice planet. Pity it's been ruined by all that fighting.'

'There is massive environmental damage,' Kelzo admits. 'Exhaust fumes from the tanks and troop vehicles have caused extensive harm to the ecosphere. In some areas of the world the robots have used nuclear weapons. The fallout has rendered those parts uninhabitable by any living organism.'

'The robots won't care, though,' you say. 'They're not people. They're just machines.'

Go to 108.

---

24 '**L**et's stay under cover for a while,' you say. 'At least until the mortar fire stops.'

Eventually it does. Tired, thirsty and covered in dust, the three of you emerge and stretch. The land all around you is a mass of churned earth and broken robots. The fighting has been intense.

Smoke rolls across the silent battlefield, and out of the murk more figures emerge — but these are not robots. They are clearly people, humans, dressed in combat fatigues and armed, but friendly.

'It's not safe out here,' the leader says. He's in his forties, grizzled and hard-looking. 'You'd better come with us.'

Go to 78.

25 | 'Nothing else for it except to walk,' the Doctor announces.

'Walk?' gasps Martha. 'We're in the middle of nowhere!'

'In that case we're exactly halfway to somewhere. Come on!'

Hands in pockets, the Doctor strolls off in a seemingly random direction. But then you realise he's seen something you and Martha haven't — a thin column of smoke on the horizon, threading its way up into the vast green sky.

It takes a while, but eventually you draw closer to the source of the smoke.

'Wonder what it is?' murmurs Martha, shielding her eyes against the sun.

'Shh,' says the Doctor, holding up a hand. 'Listen!'

'Help!'

You all hear the cry, and soon you can see a pile of twisted metal — the remains of some kind of one-man flyer by the looks of it. Lying next to it is a human girl, clearly injured.

Go to 4.

The Doctor strides over to the main control bank. The monitors flash uncertainly.

'WHAT ARE YOU DOING?' asks Machina 1.

'This was never part of your programming,' the Doctor tells the computer. 'It's got to stop — now.'

He takes out his sonic screwdriver and aims it at the control board. 'One precisely aimed sonic pulse into your CPU will shut you down forever,' the Doctor says.

'I WILL NOT ALLOW IT!'

A bolt of electrical energy surges from the computer bank and throws the Doctor across the room. He hits the rear wall and lies still, the sonic screwdriver rolling out of his limp hand.

'Doctor!' cries Martha, hurrying over to him.

You snatch up the screwdriver and aim it at the computer bank. You have one chance. You trigger the sonic pulse and the monitor screens fill with static interference. A terrible electronic squeal issues from Machina 1's speakers and the entire sky station begins to shake.

'The antigravity beams will go off-line,' the Doctor croaks. 'It's going to crash.'

Go to 107.

27 | 'War,' explains Kimer grimly. 'Never-ending war. The robots have taken over the planet — they started out fighting us... and we lost. Now they're fighting each other. The entire planet's been turned into a giant battleground.'

There is a terrible sadness in Kimer's eyes. Here is a man who has lost his entire world, in every sense. 'The robots may have taken over,' he mutters darkly, 'but they'll never wipe us out. We'll survive — whatever it takes.'

'We can do better than that,' says the Doctor. 'We can stop the robot war — forever.'

Go to 112.

---

28 | 'You CANNOT STOP ME,' booms the robotic voice. 'THIS IS OPERATIONS CONTROL. YOU ARE A LIVING ORGANISM. YOU MUST BE... TERMINATED!'

To your amazement, the Doctor simply puts his hands in his pocket and shrugs. 'Okay, do what you like. See if I care!'

The computers of Operations Control click and whirr manically — but nothing happens.

'As I thought,' the Doctor says contemptuously. 'Nothing but a pile of second-rate computers and a central communications control grid. You're powerless on your own.'

'I HAVE SUMMONED MY ROBOT GUARDS,' says the computer. 'YOU WILL BE — '

'You can't do anything!' The Doctor examines the main control panel. 'This is the nerve centre of the whole thing — the eye of the storm. We're perfectly safe here. This war's been going on and on forever — robot against robot, year after year, decade after decade. Who knows why? Maybe people wanted to settle their differences without having to fight themselves, or maybe it was just for entertainment. Or maybe all the robots just got bored and started arguing with each other. Either way, it stops — here, and now.'

Doors slide open around the perimeter of the chamber and armed robots march in.

'Here comes trouble,' says Martha.

'I don't think so.' The Doctor points to the main controls. 'That lever switches this whole thing off.' He looks at you and winks. 'Fancy it?'

Go to 54.

The Doctor opens the cell door with the screwdriver. Predictably, the robot guard is waiting for you outside.

'We're ready to talk,' says the Doctor brightly.

'TALK?'

The Doctor sighs. 'Just take us to your leader.'

'LEADER?'

'Do I have to draw a diagram?' The Doctor sounds exasperated. 'This is Machina 1! The entire sky station — it's one giant computer controlling the lot of you. Now — take me to the communications interface. Chop chop!'

The robot leads you to a large chamber lined with enormous flashing computer banks.

'I AM MACHINA 1,' the computer announces grandly.

'Yeah, thought as much.' The Doctor leans nonchalantly against a data bank. 'Nice set-up — but at the end of the day you're just a computer. Following orders.'

The computer's response is implacable. 'I FOLLOW MY PROGRAMMING.'

Go to 26.

You crawl down the left-hand shaft until you reach a grille set in the floor. A moment's work with the sonic screwdriver opens it and you all climb gratefully out.

You are in some sort of large control centre. Computer banks and machinery hum in a sterile white room. There are no guard robots here. In fact, it seems surprisingly peaceful, considering what you've been through to get here.

'Welcome to Machina 1,' says a smooth and calm voice behind you. You all whirl around to see a slender white robot hovering in the air, moving silently on anti-gravity rays.

The Doctor holds out a hand. 'Hello! I'm the Doctor, this is Martha, and this is…'

'I know who you are,' interrupts the robot, gliding forward. 'I have been monitoring your progress ever since you arrived on the planet Titanius.'

The Doctor frowns. 'Have you indeed?'

'I am Kelzo,' the robot continues. 'It is my duty to monitor the long battle below.'

Go to 23.

31 The flyer hits the ground with a terrific crash, just as you dive for safety. The machine explodes and the Doctor is flung headlong into the dirt.

Dazed, you crawl across to him. He's lying completely still.

Martha kneels down beside him. 'Doctor?'

'They say any landing you can walk away from is a good one,' the Doctor suddenly says. He sits up and ruffles his spiky hair. 'I wonder if I can walk?'

Relieved, you and Martha help him to his feet. All of you are covered in cuts and bruises and smudges of soot.

'What now?' you wonder. You're stuck in the middle of the desert, miles from anywhere.

Go to 25.

32 | Martha turns and sprints. The robot lunges for her but misses — just. The sudden move gives you a chance to run as well. Tearing free, you race in the opposite direction as a huge explosion blows you off your feet. You have no time to think of what might have happened to Martha — or even the Doctor — as more explosions roar around you.

Desperately you crawl through the dirt and then tumble into a deep, muddy trench.

If you decide to lie low in the trench until the barrage stops, go to 43. If you think you should keep moving and see where the trench leads, go to 44.

33 The whole area is rocked by the blast. For long, precious seconds you can't hear a thing and the smoke blinds you.

Someone grabs your arm. Your watering eyes focus on the Doctor; he's staring at you, saying something. Gradually your senses begin to recover and you can just about hear him yelling, 'Sorry about that! No time for a proper warning!'

You stagger to your feet, coughing up dust. Your skin stings where bits of shrapnel have struck. At your feet are the remains of the robot. Above you is the open sky — the explosion has ripped the bunker wide open.

'Where's Martha?' you ask.

'Here,' she says, grabbing your hand. 'Come on — we've got to get away from here.'

Together you climb out of the crater.

Go to 45.

34 As you run out of the crater, the air is filled with the roar of aircraft low overhead. A small, chunky-looking plane shoots over the rim of the crater followed by a jet fighter.

'Down!' cries the Doctor, pushing Martha to the floor. You dive for cover as a hail of gunfire shatters the air and the remains of the jet cartwheel across the green sky, trailing fire and smoke until they meet the ground with a splintering crash.

'The other one's down as well,' you say.

'Let's go and have a look,' suggests Martha.

Go to 45.

35 The fierce sounds of battle are drawing ever closer.

'Back to the TARDIS, then,' orders the Doctor, clambering over the twisted debris as a high whistling noise fills the air. 'Hurry up — *incoming!*'

You race with Martha towards the police box, but a series of deafening explosions pound the crater ridge and you are flung off your feet. When the vibrations stop, you can see Martha lying a few feet away. There is a bruise on her forehead where a piece of flying metal has struck her a glancing blow.

You can't see the Doctor or the TARDIS through the swirling fog of dust.

Martha's eyes flicker open. She looks dazed. 'Go and find the Doctor,' she urges.

If you want to look for the Doctor, go to 77. If you stay to help Martha yourself, go to 7.

36 | The Doctor has the manhole cover open in a moment using the sonic screwdriver. 'I'll go first,' he says, 'then Martha and you. Stay quiet and above all don't panic. It's going to be dark down there.'

With a cheery grin he starts to climb down a metal ladder set into the side of the shaft. 'I don't think this is one of your best ideas, Doctor,' Martha whispers as you both follow him. 'It's not only dark down here — it's cold and wet too. And it reminds me of New York...'

The Doctor's produced a torch from one of his coat pockets. As you reach the bottom of the ladder, he's shining the beam around a small concrete chamber. The floor's swilling with grimy water and a rat scuttles into the shadows.

'Shh,' the Doctor whispers. 'Listen!'

There are voices coming from the darkness up ahead — a tunnel of some kind.

If you think you should follow the voices, go to 48. If you think you should hide, go to 49.

37 | 'I don't fancy any more sewers,' says Martha. 'I had enough of them in New York!'

You all agree to move on — the sounds of battle are growing closer again. Gunfire and explosions are a never-ending background noise on this planet.

Soon you discover a narrow ditch that leads to a deep trench. You follow the Doctor and Martha into the trench, but the soft ground crumbles and gives way. You tumble down in a shower of loose soil, coughing and spluttering.

When you recover, there's no sign of your friends. Smoke drifts through the trench and, to your horror, you find a number of dead human soldiers lying in the mud.

Then you see the robot.

At first you think it's about to attack, but then you realise that it's inactive. The light has faded from its eyes and it topples over in front of you.

Go to 81.

38 'If you're in control up here,' you say, 'then you should stop it.'

'I cannot stop it,' Kelzo replies calmly. 'It is against my programming.'

'Then your programming is going to have to change,' says Martha firmly.

Kelzo turns towards her. With a quiet hum, the robot's hands split open to reveal two whirring laser blades. It begins to glide menacingly towards her. 'The war must continue!'

'Martha, get down!' the Doctor launches himself across the control room, diving at Martha. Together they hit the polished white floor and skid across to the main control computer. The Doctor leaps up and begins to press every switch he can find. 'Quick!' he shouts. 'The controls — activate them all!'

You and Martha immediately begin hitting buttons and twisting controls. You find a bank of levers and push them all in random directions.

Behind you, Kelzo has an electronic seizure — sparks fly out of his casing and smoke begins to pour from his head. 'Leave the controls!' the robot screams, and then, with a sudden crackle of energy, wires and circuits spew out of his head and the control room is filled with the smell of burning.

Go to 75.

A little later you materialise back on the planet.

'There!' announces the Doctor, satisfied. 'Not a bad morning's work — interminable war stopped, friends made, everyone happy.'

'And so nice of Kelzo to teleport us straight back to the TARDIS,' Martha notes, tapping the police box affectionately.

'Oh, yes. Good old Kelzo!'

'What will happen to him?' you wonder.

The Doctor opens the TARDIS door and ushers you inside. 'Well I added a few extras to his programming,' he chuckles. 'Soon he'll make all the robots start repairing the damage they've done over the centuries.'

'We should pop back again in a few years' time,' suggests Martha as you gather around the control console. 'See how they're getting on.'

'Maybe we will,' the Doctor smiles, pulling the dematerialisation lever. 'Maybe we will...'

THE END

40 Without a word you dip your hand into the Doctor's jacket pocket and find the sonic screwdriver. You pass the device to the Doctor. The nearest robot swivels its head to look directly at you but your face is a picture of innocence.

It only takes a moment's work for the Doctor to release the handcuffs. He winks at you and pockets the screwdriver as the robot marches stiffly over.

'WHAT ARE YOU DOING?'

'Nothing,' replies the Doctor. 'Why, what are *you* doing?'

The robot stares at him blankly, and then, quite suddenly, its head blows off in a shower of sparks. The body stands there for a second, wavering — you can't take your eyes off the nest of wires poking out of the neck — and then it collapses at your feet.

You pick up the robot's skull and look at the Doctor — the sonic screwdriver? But he shakes his head. 'Not me.'

If you decide to take your chance and make a run for it with the Doctor, go to 55. If you think you should examine the robot more closely, go to 56.

41 | 'I can't,' you whisper. 'Too risky.'

The Doctor nods. 'OK — it'll wait. Anyway, it looks like we've got company.'

A military truck on caterpillar tracks is rumbling up to the holding post. There are more robots on-board — along with Martha.

'I thought you'd hurt your leg,' you say as the truck pulls up in a cloud of dirty exhaust.

'Walking wounded,' Martha replies with a brave smile. 'Nice to see you guys, anyway. Hey — look what the cat's dragged in!'

She's pointing to another, larger truck as it pulls up alongside. Mounted on the back of it is none other than the TARDIS.

Go to 68.

'It's all right,' Martha calls out. 'There's nothing we can do against these things. Best just to give ourselves up — for now.'

You see the defiant glint in her eye and nod. Another robot hurls you roughly towards Martha.

'YOU WILL BE TAKEN FOR ANALYSIS,' announces of one the other robots.

You are made to stand on a small flying platform with a kind of handrail — it's the only thing to grab on to, and the only thing that will stop you falling off. The flyer's engine cranks up to a loud whine and suddenly you're in the air. The robot pilot guides the vehicle up over the battlefield; it's a long way down and all you can see is miles of desert scarred by continuous mechanical carnage.

Suddenly the flyer veers to the left and you have to tighten your grip. You look at Martha — she's seen something and she looks scared. You twist around, scanning the air around you. What has she seen?

Go to 59.

43 Keeping very still, you wait for the barrage to stop. Eventually the guns cease, although you can still hear the sounds of battle in the distance. On this planet the fighting never seems to stop.

Cautiously, you climb out of the trench and take a look around.

The robots have moved on. Smoke drifts across the churned-up mud like ghosts. As you watch and listen you become aware of a strange mechanical whine, like a motor left idling.

You spot an abandoned vehicle. It looks like some sort of flying machine — a small platform big enough for two or three people, with stubby wings and a handrail. The engine is still running.

It's too good an opportunity to miss. If you can get airborne you can look for the Doctor and Martha more easily.

But as you approach the flyer, something moves behind it — something's been hiding there, just out of view...

If you move forward to see what it is, go to 60. If you think you should back off, go to 61.

Every instinct tells you to keep moving. Crawling along through the freezing mud on all fours, you explore the trench. Because of the smoke you can only see a few metres ahead, but you want to find out what's just around the corner.

When you turn the corner, you wish you hadn't.

There are bodies here. The first one you find is a robot, similar to the first one you saw — except that its head is dangling from its shoulders by a couple of thick, charred wires and the eyes are dark.

The second body is a human being dressed in muddy combat fatigues. He's clearly been dead for sometime.

If this puts you off and you think you should go back, go to 61. If you think this is good because it means there are human beings around, go to 62.

45 'This way,' shouts the Doctor. About a hundred metres to your left is some sort of vehicle lying in the dirt.

The Doctor runs across to the machine. When you and Martha catch up you find the Doctor already on his knees with the sonic screwdriver out.

'Some sort of short-distance aircraft,' explains the Doctor. You can see now that the vehicle is a sturdy, speedboat-shaped platform with stubby wings and powerful engines.

'And it's still in working order,' announces the Doctor, completing his examination. 'No sign of any pilot either, so it's finders keepers! All aboard!'

'Hang on,' says Martha. 'Where are you thinking of going? And where's the TARDIS?'

If you think you might be able to spot the TARDIS from the air, go to 63. If you think you should avoid using the flyer, go to 64.

46 You run after Martha, but you're soon lost in the smoke. The gunfire eventually stops and you collapse to your knees. It's hopeless. You have no idea which direction to take. You're on your own.

'No time for sitting around,' says a friendly voice, and a hand lifts you to your feet. It's the Doctor! 'Can't find Martha anywhere,' he says, 'but at least I've got you.'

'We were separated!' you gasp. 'I couldn't tell which way you went.'

The Doctor shrugs. 'Martha's very resourceful.' He sounds unconcerned, but you can see the worry in his dark eyes.

He points to the rucksack you're still carrying. 'Let's take a look at that again,' he says.

Go to 56.

47 Almost paralysed with fear, you throw your hands up in the air. Startled, the Doctor does the same. 'Yeah — great idea,' he nods. 'Martha — hands up.'

Slowly Martha raises her hands as well.

'YOU WILL BE TAKEN FOR ANALYSIS,' says the leading robot. All three of you march out of the crater, and you take the chance to check that you really have done the right thing.

'I dunno,' admits the Doctor quietly. 'At the very least it's bought us some time.'

'The only alternative was being shot,' Martha adds. 'So I prefer this any day.'

You now have a view of the planet — a mountainous world of ragged, torn battlefields, pockmarked with countless craters and charred wreckage. The air reeks of machine oil and hot metal.

Parked nearby is a large, rusty flatbed truck mounted on huge caterpillar tracks. Thick black smoke belches from a chimney of exhaust pipes. On the back of the truck is the TARDIS, guarded by another robot.

If you make a dash for the TARDIS, go to 67. If you pretend not to recognise it, go to 68.

48 'They're human voices,' you say quietly. 'We should introduce ourselves.'

The Doctor nods. 'Hello!' he calls out into the darkness, his voice echoing off the damp brickwork. 'Anyone at home?'

'Hold it right there,' orders a gruff voice. The Doctor's torch settles on a group of soldiers aiming automatic laser weapons at you. The leader of the men, a tall, tough-looking man in combat fatigues, moves forward. 'Put the torch down!' he says, levelling a heavy pistol at the Doctor.

'It's all right,' the Doctor replies amiably. 'We're not here to fight. Anyone know a Tela?'

'Tela?' echoes the man. 'Where is she?'

'She's dead,' Martha says sadly. 'She was killed in a bomb blast after her flyer came down.'

'Casualty of war,' replies the soldier gruffly. 'Now what are you lot doing down here?'

Go to 69.

'**Q**uick, hide!' The three of you squeeze into a small alcove hidden in the shadows on one side of the tunnel. You hardly dare to breath. You strain to listen for the sounds but the echoes in the passageway make it very difficult.

And there's a rat climbing over your left foot.

You look down and freeze. The grimy rodent scuttles around your ankles, its tail dragging behind it. Martha's seen it too — you can feel her fingers digging into your arm!

Trying to ignore the rat, you concentrate on the voices. They seem to be getting nearer. It might be important to hear what they have to say — but it could be dangerous if you're discovered.

If you think you should stay and listen, go to 48. If you think you should get away while you still can, go to 12.

You may end up trapped in this trench. Time to move out.

You're covered in mud and filthy from the sewer, so you'll be pretty hard to spot. Carefully, you crawl out of the ditch. Keeping low and moving slowly, you circle around the back of the robot platoon. They have broken ranks to engage the enemy on the far ridge — explosive rounds are throwing up chunks of dirt all around and laser bolts zip back and forth.

You have no idea what direction to take — until you hear a friendly voice hissing, 'Oi! Over here!'

Two figures are waving at you from behind a pile of rocks. It's the Doctor and Martha! They must have escaped the tunnels as well!

'I've an idea how to stop all this,' the Doctor says as you join them. 'But we need Grant Kimer's help.'

'But we can't go back!' argues Martha. 'Those robot dogs will tear us to pieces!'

If you think you should get away from the battle first, go to 101. If you think you should double back to find Grant Kimer, go to 76.

'We can't come all this way and not have a look around first,' you say. 'I mean — alien planet! Travelling through time and space — this is what I love!'

Martha shrugs and looks at the Doctor. 'Kid's got it bad.'

'Righto,' the Doctor nods, hands in pockets. 'Just a quick look around, mind. I don't enjoy war zones as a rule.'

You wander up to the rim of the crater and have your first proper view of this new world. Under the deep green sky, all you can see is a desert churned by constant battle. You can see the wrecks of armoured vehicles and tanks — some of them are enormous. All of them are shattered, some still on fire, bleeding thick black smoke.

'Help!'

You all hear the cry. Not far away there's a pile of twisted metal — the remains of some sort of one-man flyer by the looks of it. Lying next to it is a human girl, clearly injured.

If you immediately run to help, go to 5. If you wait to see what the Doctor advises, go to 4.

'This way!' says the Doctor, hurrying to the right. You follow him to another junction and a small doorway. He has it open in a second and you rush through to a larger chamber, full of computer banks and sterile white instrumentation. It's quite a contrast to the battle-ravaged planet below. On monitor screens you can see what's happening on every battlefield — robot after robot destroying other robots in an endless scene of mechanical carnage.

'This is insane,' the Doctor murmurs grimly. 'Someone — or something — is responsible for this.'

'I AM RESPONSIBLE!' booms a loud, electronic voice.

The voice seems to come from everywhere. The lights on the computers flash in time with the words.

'Oh, I get it,' says the Doctor. 'This is Machina 1 — this whole sky station. Hovering over the planet below, making sure the war of the robots never ends.'

'IT MUST NOT END.'

'Why not?' the Doctor demands, his voice rising angrily. 'What's it *for*?'

'IT IS FOR MY AMUSEMENT,' replies Machina 1. 'I HAVE OUTLIVED THE HUMAN BEINGS WHO CREATED ME BY A THOUSAND YEARS — BUT I AM BORED. I MAKE THE ROBOTS

FIGHT EACH OTHER FOR MY ENTERTAINMENT.'

'Entertainment?' echoes Martha in disbelief. 'You call that entertainment?'

'Couldn't you have just read a book or something?' asks the Doctor. 'No — don't answer that. It's a joke — and I've never met a computer that could get a joke. Because that's all you are — a jumped-up computer with time on its hands and nothing to compute.'

'We've got to stop it — all those robots fighting each other...' Martha says, 'It's stupid and unnecessary.'

The Doctor looks at her. 'They're not alive. They don't feel anything.'

'I know, but I still feel sort of sorry for them. They can't help it, can they?'

'No. But *we* can. And so can Machina I.'

Go to 26.

'Run!' you yell. You're just under the range of the shoulder-blaster's pivot. It tries to aim at you but the shot goes wild. As the robot whirls to adjust its aim, the Doctor slips behind it and fiddles with something behind the machine's head. Suddenly, with a dying whine of internal motors, the robot stops moving.

'What did you do?' Martha asks.

'The robot has an Achilles' neck,' the Doctor jokes, brandishing his sonic screwdriver. 'I've paralysed its central computer junction — but only temporarily. The effect won't last long.'

'Then let's get moving,' you say.

'Hang on a mo... I've just had an idea!' The Doctor does some more work with the sonic screwdriver and removes a chunky component from the robot's head. 'If I can boost the screwdriver's sonic pulse through the robot's communication network, I should be able to paralyse the entire army. It's just a case of getting the right trigger signal...'

A minute later, the Doctor replaces the robot's computer brain and reactivates it. The robot stiffens and jerks — and a web of blue lines suddenly shoot from its antennae, spreading right across the battlefield, connecting with all the other robots.

'Each robot will receive the signal and send it on,' the Doctor beams. 'The paralysis will spread right across the planet!'

Go to 109.

54 With a grin you pull the lever. The power dies with a whine, the lights on the computers blinking out one by one, and the advancing robots shudder to a halt.

There's an eerie silence.

'What's happened to all the robots?' asks Martha. 'They've stopped fighting.'

'They were controlled by this central computer,' explains the Doctor happily. 'All we had to do was switch it off and the whole thing stops. The robot war is over. I'll send a message to the Galactic Authorities, let them know the planet's safe. Can't just leave the place to rust forever, can we?'

'In that case,' says Martha, 'it's time we left. Didn't you say something about a holiday? Somewhere warm and sunny...?'

'After you,' says the Doctor, unlocking the TARDIS.

You follow Martha inside, and soon the TARDIS is on its way to new times and places...

THE END

55 | 'Come on,' says the Doctor, 'we'd better get out of here!'

Together you turn to run, but there are some men walking towards you. They're dressed in combat fatigues and they're carrying weapons.

'What are you doing out here in the open?' demands the leader. He's rough-looking, aged about forty. The rifle he carries is smoking, and it's obvious that it was he who shot the robot's head off.

But you've seen someone limping along with the soldiers — Martha!

You and the Doctor rush over to greet her.

'We found this girl injured in a crater,' explains the soldier gruffly. 'It's a miracle you're all still alive! You'd better come with us.'

Go to 78.

56 'Let's see what's in here,' suggests the Doctor, opening up the metal skull. 'Ah — just as I thought. Coaxial link to the communications network. Could be useful!'

You don't really know what he's talking about — but that hardly matters now. A shadow falls over you and you look up to find a group of armed humans covering you with automatic laser weapons. But there's someone else with them that you recognise.

'Martha!'

She introduces you to her new friends — the only surviving humans on this planet. Their world has been turned upside down by an uncontrollable robot war.

'We'd noticed,' says the Doctor. 'But this might help.' He holds up the component from the robot's computer brain.

'You could be right,' says the leader of the humans, Grant Kimer. He eyes the Doctor carefully. 'We'd best get underground though — for your own safety.'

Kimer's men lead the three of you down a nearby manhole cover into a small underground chamber.

Go to 89.

57 'We'd better keep moving,' you say. The Doctor and Martha nod and follow you out from under the rocks, keeping low as they run. Aircraft roar overhead, firing missiles into the earth below. On the horizon, enormous tanks churn up clouds of dust with huge caterpillar tracks.

'This way!' screams Martha over the noise. She's seen something away to the left.

Suddenly a volley of laser beams turns the sand around you into globules of molten glass. You slip and hit the ground hard. For a second you're stunned. You see the Doctor and Martha running off in different directions.

If you get back on your feet and chase after Martha, go to 46. If you get back on your feet and chase after the Doctor, go to 79.

58 'It's no good,' Martha yells. 'We're going down!'

The robot squadron peels away and roars into the distance as your flyer plummets towards the desert below. But then you see another flyer, alone, zooming up behind you. At the controls is a strangely familiar figure — tall, skinny, with a long coat flapping like wings in the slipstream.

'Hello there!' calls the Doctor, pulling up alongside your flyer.

'Doctor!' Martha shouts. 'We're going to crash!'

'Hang on!' The Doctor carefully pulls his flyer under yours and, with supreme skill, manages to keep it level — but not enough to prevent a hard landing! The flyer skims across the earth with a series of sickening jolts before turning on its side. You and Martha are thrown clear but you are still alive.

'Uh oh,' gasps Martha, looking up at the Doctor's flyer. It's pitched too far to port and the antigravity rays have cut out completely. The tiny craft is suddenly plunging towards you.

'Look out!' yells the Doctor.

Go to 31.

59 'Look out!' Martha screams over the wind.

More robot flyers are coming into attack, flying in formation, guns blazing.

Your robot pilot's seen them too. It operates the controls with infuriating calm, sending the flyer veering this way and that, threatening to throw Martha and you off if you don't hold on tight enough.

Laser bolts burn through the air around you. One punches a hole through the deck plate at your feet. Another splits the robot pilot's head in half, showering you with sparks. Gradually the robot slides away and disappears over the edge of the flyer, trailing oil.

Go to 115.

---

60 A small figure stands up. It's Martha.

'There you are!' she gasps, running towards you. 'Thank goodness you're safe. We thought we'd lost you.'

'Where's the Doctor?' you ask.

Her face falls. 'I don't know. We got separated when we ran. I don't know if he got away or not.'

'This looks like it could be useful,' you say, giving the flyer a kick. 'If we can get it up, we can search for the Doctor.'

'I don't know,' Martha sounds dubious. 'It could be dangerous.'

'Everything here is dangerous,' you point out. 'Even standing here talking. The battle could come this way, we could be spotted by other flyers, or a bomb could drop and blow us both to pieces.'

Martha nods and smiles. 'You're right. What's a bit of danger between friends, anyway? Let's go for it!'

You both jump on to the flyer. The controls are simple and obvious. After a few seconds, you've got the machine rising into the air at a fantastic rate. In a minute you can see the entire battlefield — churned desert, pockmarked with craters and littered with the debris of a massive war, stretching as far as the eye can see. It is horrendous.

'We'll never find the Doctor like this,' Martha yells over the roar of the wind.

'Wait a minute,' you reply, pointing. 'What's that…?'

Go to 88.

61 Scared, you back away. Slowly at first, but then hurriedly...

Right into a robot.

You whirl around, looking up at the towering metal figure. Its burning green eyes stare down at you for several long seconds.

But it doesn't move.

Then, gradually, the emerald glow in its eyes begins to fade. The whine of motors within the armoured torso dies and the robot slowly topples over. You scramble out of the way as the machine hits the ground with a loud rattle.

It doesn't move again.

Breathing hard you stare into the swirling mist, trying to see what took the robot out like that...

Go to 81.

As horrible a sight as this is, it does mean one thing: at least there are other human beings here. Or at least there were.

Gritting your teeth, you carefully climb over the robot and the corpse. You wonder if they died killing each other — the human was armed with some kind of heavy rifle; you can see it lying in the muck by his feet.

Cautiously you move forward in a low crouch. The sound of the battle has faded a little. But there is still no sign of the Doctor or Martha.

Suddenly you hear voices up ahead. You can't see who it is around the bend in the trench, and you can't hear what they're saying — but it's definitely a man and a woman.

If you call out to see if it's the Doctor and Martha, go to 81. If you're taking no chances and pick up the fallen gun, go to 96.

63 'We might be able to spot the TARDIS from the air,' you say. 'At the very least we could get a good look at what's going on.'

The Doctor climbs on to the platform of the flyer and inspects the controls. 'Should be pretty simple. If a robot can fly it then I'm sure we can.'

'Maybe it only works for robots,' you tell him.

'You're right,' he says, tapping the control panel. 'I could hot-wire it, though!' He pulls out his sonic screwdriver and sets to work.

If the Doctor gets the flyer to work, go to 82. If the flyer won't work, go to 83.

64 'Wait,' you say. 'That thing was built for the robots to use. It could be booby-trapped.'

'Good point,' grins the Doctor. 'I like you!' He scans the flyer once more with his sonic screwdriver and nods. 'You're spot on — the power rods are set to implode if any organic being steps on-board. Good job we've got you, isn't it?'

You can feel yourself blushing as Martha smiles at you.

'Well, we can't just stand around here clapping you on the back and saying how clever you are, can we?' adds the Doctor. You can all hear the sound of gunfire drawing closer. 'Somehow we've got to get to whoever or whatever is directing this war. We're too exposed out here in the middle of the battlefield. Any suggestions?'

If you suggest walking to the next rise to see what's over there, go to 83. If you think you should search the surrounding area for the TARDIS, go to 65.

65 | Smoke drifts across the crater while you think about what to do next. The Doctor and Martha walk towards you.

'I thought we could look for the TARDIS,' you tell them. 'Once we've found it we can plan what to do next.'

'That might be difficult,' Martha says, 'the whole place is crawling with robots.'

'We're slap bang in the middle of a war,' agrees the Doctor. 'We may not be so lucky the next time we're found.'

'I wonder what started it all?' says Martha.

The Doctor shrugs, hands in pockets. 'What starts any war? Usually someone or something being unreasonable. Once you can't reason with someone, it always gets ugly. But robots don't usually fight unless they're programmed to.'

'So we need to find who's doing the programming?' you venture.

'That'll do for starters,' the Doctor grins, moving off into the drifting smoke. 'Come on, you two!'

Go to 84.

You see the green eyes glowing through the fog and immediately turn to run. But coming the other way are the hulking shapes of two more robots. Their eyes follow you through the mist as you turn this way and that, looking for somewhere to run. Perhaps making a break for it was a bad idea.

Laser beams rip through the air and the first robot staggers back. Sparks fly and the machine collapses in a swirl of dust.

More laser bolts tear into the other robots. They start to raise their own weapons but the damage has already been done; smoke pouring from their joints, the machines grind to a halt and the light fades from their eyes.

You've been caught in the crossfire; more robots appear over the rise, scanning the area with their weapons. They see you.

Go to 85.

67 You gasp with relief at the sight of the old police box and immediately run towards it.

'HALT!' cries one of the robots, levelling its gun.

'Wait!' yells the Doctor. 'Stop!'

You roll to one side as the robot fires, laser beams kicking up earth where you stood a moment ago. The Doctor and Martha dive for cover and you roll underneath the flatbed truck. You can hear the robots clanking around as you scramble through the dirt beneath the vehicle and jump to your feet on the other side. The Doctor and Martha are shouting, distracting the robots, and you feel a surge of hope. Clambering up onto the back of the truck, you rest your hands gratefully on the warm wooden exterior of the TARDIS.

Only then do you realise you haven't got a key.

The Doctor and Martha are now standing with their hands on their heads, guarded by robots. No one knows where you've gone. The robots are stomping around searching for you.

If you make a run for it in the hope of getting help, go to 85. If you give yourself up, go to 86.

You almost gasp with relief at the sight of the old police box, but the Doctor shoots you a warning look. Biting your lip, you nod and keep quiet.

'GET ON THE TRUCK,' orders the robot behind you with a prod of its gun. You help Martha on-board. The Doctor pointedly ignores the TARDIS as he turns to your captors.

'Where are we off to then?' he asks.

'YOU WILL BE TAKEN TO STATION 7X FOR ANALYSIS AND TRANSFER.'

'Sounds lovely! Any chance of a cup of tea and a biscuit?'

'NONE.'

'Thought not.'

The truck's heavy motors rumble into life and a cloud of choking fumes spurts from the exhausts. With a grinding roar the great caterpillar tracks bite into the rubble and the vehicle lurches forward.

Bombs explode on the horizon as the truck trundles across the battlefield until it reaches the entrance to a concrete bunker guarded by robot dogs. Their metallic jaws snap at you as the robots march you towards the bunker. The TARDIS is driven away on the truck and you wonder if you will ever see it again.

At the entrance to the bunker you are made to stand with your hands on your head. 'ONE OF YOU WILL ENTER FIRST,' orders the robot.

If you volunteer to go first, go to 95. If you wait to see if anyone else volunteers, go to 105.

'We're travellers,' you blurt. 'We're here by accident. This is the Doctor and Martha. I'm...'

'I'm not interested in your names,' replies the man. 'Unless you want them written on your gravestones.'

'I think we're jumping the gun a bit here,' says the Doctor. He reaches forward and gently pushes the laser pistol aside. 'There's no need for all that. You can see we're not armed.'

The man nods. 'I suppose. But what's that you've got?'

He's pointing to the rucksack you're carrying. 'It was Tela's,' you tell him.

'She gave it to us,' says Martha. 'She seemed to think it was important.'

The man takes the rucksack and examines the contents. His weathered features show some surprise. 'This could be just what we're looking for. You'd better come with us!'

Go to 89

'Hold on a minute,' you say. 'I've got a few questions. Like — what's going on here? Who are you? And what's this 'long battle' all about?'

Martha nods and the Doctor folds his arms, looking at the white robot. 'Yeah, Kelzo. What's it all about?'

'For centuries the robots have fought each other for control of Titanius,' Kelzo replies calmly. 'It is my job to monitor their progress.'

'But what started the war?' Martha asks. 'Why all that fighting and destruction? What's the point?'

'The war robots and I were created thousands of years ago by human beings. The robots were intended to fight on the humans' behalf, but there are very few humans still alive now and the robots were left to continue the war.'

'Because they didn't know what else to do?'

'Precisely.'

If you think Kelzo could stop the war, go to 38. If you think you need to learn more, go to 23.

71 'Wait a moment,' says the Doctor, moving slowly towards the robot hound.

'Be careful!' Martha warns. 'That thing's got jaws like a steel trap!'

'I'm pretty good with robot dogs,' smiles the Doctor. He kneels down slowly in front of the snarling machine. 'Hello there. Who's a good boy then?'

The robot whines and its head droops heavily. The sound of rust scraping in its internal gears is excruciating. Large globs of thick, dirty oil drip from its fangs.

'You're not very well, are you?' the Doctor asks gently. 'I think he's been put in here on guard duty and forgotten about. The poor thing's corroded beyond repair. He's barely functional.'

The Doctor presses his sonic screwdriver to the side of the machine's head. Slowly, with an ominous creak, the robot keels over.

'What have you done?' you ask.

'Put it to sleep,' the Doctor replies grimly. 'Come on — look what the poor thing's been guarding all this time.'

On the floor is a manhole cover.

Go to 103.

The robot's grip is incredibly strong — but not lethal.

'Don't struggle,' orders the Doctor. 'Let's see what it wants…'

The robot fixes you with a steady green glare. Guns mounted near the machine's head swivel menacingly. 'YOU CANNOT STOP THE WAR OF THE ROBOTS,' it informs you bleakly. 'WE ALL SHARE THE SAME PROGRAMMING.'

'That's all very useful,' replies the Doctor. 'But there are better programs than war.'

'SUCH AS?'

'Well there's one, straight off — *curiosity*. Interest. You haven't killed us outright… You want to learn — which means you want to change, to adapt. There's no future in war — you must know that.'

'WHAT ELSE IS THERE?'

If you think there's no hope and you must fight on, go to 53. If you think there's a chance of persuading the robot to stop, go to 113.

73 Taking stock of the situation, you find yourselves standing in the middle of a silent battleground. The area is littered with the blazing wrecks of tanks and broken robots.

Walking towards you is a group of men — humans — in combat fatigues. They look war-torn and tired, covered in grime and sweat. They're armed, but they are looking at you curiously.

'I'm Grant Kimer,' says the leader, a tall man in his late forties with a scar down one side of his face. 'We're the last humans alive on this planet — or at least, we thought we were.'

The Doctor introduces you all and hands over Tela's rucksack. 'We found Tela — she said to give this to you.'

Kimer is grateful. 'This should help us find the location of the Omnipus,' he says, and then, catching your puzzled look, adds, 'The giant robot rumoured to control everything on this planet.'

'Actually,' the Doctor says with a smile, 'We're visitors here… can you tell us just what, exactly, is going on?'

Go to 27.

A little later, you're all standing by the TARDIS. Martha is saying goodbye to Grant Kimer, and the Doctor is speaking to Titanius.

The giant metal Omnipus towers over the Doctor.

'YOU HAVE STOPPED THE WAR OF THE ROBOTS, DOCTOR,' Titanius booms.

'Not me,' replies the Doctor. 'You did it — you're the one in control. All I did was remove the inhibitor circuit that prevented you from overriding the robots' control program.'

'BUT WHAT ABOUT THE HUMANS?'

Kimer stands next to the Doctor. 'Maybe we can come to some sort of understanding?'

'Kimer needs you and the robots to help rebuild this world,' says the Doctor. 'You need him and his people to keep you properly maintained. How about it?'

The Doctor walks away as Kimer and Titanius begin to talk.

'Can't we stay and see what happens?' wonders Martha as he unlocks the door of the TARDIS.

'Best not,' the Doctor smiles and winks at you. 'We can always imagine, can't we?'

And soon the TARDIS is fading away, bound for new adventures...

THE END

The computer bank starts to fizz and crackle.

'This whole place is going to explode,' the Doctor shouts. 'Come on! This way!'

He leads you to a small cubicle at the rear of the room and ushers you inside.

'What's this?' asks Martha. 'Power shower?'

'Emergency teleport,' he says hurriedly, fingers flying over the controls. 'Bit like a lifeboat. Only better.'

He pulls out his sonic screwdriver and activates the teleport by remote control...

A second later the three of you are standing next to the TARDIS, back on the surface of the planet. 'Oh, right on target!' the Doctor exclaims triumphantly.

There's an eerie silence.

'What's happened to all the robots?' asks Martha. 'They've stopped fighting.'

'They were all controlled by Kelzo,' explains the Doctor happily. 'Once he blew a fuse, the whole thing ground to a halt. The robot war is over.'

'In that case,' says Martha, 'it's time we left. Didn't you say something about a holiday? Somewhere warm and sunny...?'

'After you,' says the Doctor, unlocking the TARDIS.

You follow Martha inside, and soon the TARDIS is on its way to new times and places...

THE END

---

76 'This way,' says the Doctor, leading you out into the open. 'Kimer won't be far.'

The human leader is sitting against a rock, holding his arm. His sleeve is torn and the flesh beneath has been mauled by a robot dog. 'Thing nearly took my hand off,' he mutters as you approach.

Martha tends the wound. 'That'll teach you to pat a strange dog.'

Kimer smiles weakly. 'Can we really stop the robots, Doctor?'

'Well, we could...' the Doctor agrees, 'if it wasn't for the rather large and unfriendly robot pointing a gun at us right now.'

He raises his hands as you all turn to see the robot approach...

Go to 110.

You scramble out of the crater and see a planet decimated by warfare. As far as the eye can see, there is nothing but churned mud, scarred wreckage and drifting smoke. The sound of gunfire is constant, and there is an acrid stench of burning oil and scorched metal. But there's no sign of the Doctor.

You are about to turn and run back to Martha when something bursts out of the mud at your feet. Covered in grime, a humanoid figure emerges like a corpse from a grave — but beneath the dirt, you can see burnished metal and a tangle of wires and pistons. Green eyes glow in a metallic face.

It's some kind of robot.

It raises a large, heavy rifle and aims it right at your head.

'ALL HUMANS MUST DIE!' it proclaims in a harsh, steely voice.

Go to 8.

'I'm Grant Kimer,' says the leader of the men when you reach his nearby camp. His men are a rag-tag collection of human survivors.

'The robots have done everything they can to wipe us out,' Kimer explains. 'And we've done everything we can to survive. But we can't go on much longer. We're running out of laser charges for our guns and the robots aren't easy to stop.'

'I'm sure we can think of something,' says the Doctor. 'Look at this, for instance...' He's holding up a robot's head — it's dented and rusted and horribly familiar. 'Someone went to a great deal of trouble to keep this head intact — and to make sure it got back to Grant Kimer.' The Doctor scans the decapitated metal skull with the sonic screwdriver. 'If we can trace the control signal on this robot's brain, we could locate the master control centre.'

'You mean whoever's in charge of all the robots?' asks Martha.

'Or whatever's in charge...'

'But what if whoever or whatever is controlling the robots can trace us here using the same signal?' you ask.

'That's a good point,' the Doctor muses, studying the inside of the robot's head through his glasses. 'Ah — it's just as

I thought: Multitronic code relay. All the robots are connected by a simple telecommunications signal.'

'How can that help?' you ask.

'Well if we can get to the master control, then we can stop all of the robots in their tracks — forever.'

Go to 112.

---

79 You hurry after the Doctor, although you're not certain which direction he took. It's difficult to see anything in all this smoke. After a few minutes you're totally lost.

You fall into a ditch and lie there, winded. It's wet and full of bits of broken robots and equipment. But then you find something that might be useful — a dropped laser gun. It's heavy but it looks to be in working order.

And then you hear voices up ahead — coming from around the corner of the trench.

There's no way back — if you run they'll hear you. But you do have a weapon...

Go to 96.

With a final heave you prise open the hatch, blinking as the light pours down along with flakes of rust. You clamber out of the manhole, breathing hard, and collapse.

You appear to be in some sort of ditch. The ground beneath you is very muddy — possibly it's some sort of drainage channel leading to the sewers. You crawl along the ditch for a few more metres and then stop.

You can hear the sound of gunfire from above.

Peering over the lip of the trench, you spy a platoon of heavy robots trooping past. You duck back down. The sound of gunfire is drawing closer — you've escaped from the tunnel right back into the battle!

If you think you should lie low and wait for the fighting to pass, go to 116. If you think you should take your chance and get out of the trench, go to 50.

'Doctor? Martha? Is that you?' Your shaky whisper betrays your fear. You take a step back as two figures emerge from the smoke, splashing through the trench.

'There you are!' says the Doctor brightly, pocketing his sonic screwdriver. 'Ew. You look like a drowned rat.'

'Look,' says Martha, pointing to the bodies behind you. 'They look like soldiers,' she says. 'Poor guys — killed in action, by the looks of it.'

The Doctor nods. 'Well that would make sense, we're in the middle of a war zone. But humans vs robots? There's got to be more to it than that…'

'There is,' says a gruff voice from behind the Doctor. You all turn to see a group of men in combat fatigues walking up the trench towards you. They are all armed.

'Grant Kimer,' says the leader, shaking the Doctor's hand and nodding to you and Martha. Kimer is in his mid-forties, but tough and with clear grey eyes. An old scar shows whitely on his weathered face, running from his left eye to his chin.

'You'd better come this way,' says Kimer. 'Quickly now, before the robots catch up!'

Go to 89.

82 Within moments the flyer's engines are howling and with a loud whoop of delight the Doctor has the machine airborne. Martha screams with delight as the flyer soars up into the air, but you feel as though you've left your stomach behind on the ground.

Below you can see the battlefield, stretching literally from horizon to horizon in all directions. The only landmarks are crash sites and explosions, with immense columns of black smoke rising into the sky like pillars.

In the distance you can see ranks of gigantic machines grinding across the desert. A huge cloud of dust and exhaust fumes rises in their wake. Smaller vehicles dart in and out of the tanks, and among them you can just make out the robot troops marching around.

'We'd better make ourselves scarce,' yells the Doctor, veering the flyer away from the advancing ground forces.

The flyer dips and you grip the handrail tighter.

'Whoa!' shouts Martha.

'Look out!' cries the Doctor. 'I can't pull her out of the dive!'

If you think the flyer's going to crash, go to 31. If you think you can pull it out of the dive, go to 92.

'All right,' agrees the Doctor. 'So it won't work. We'll have to hoof it instead!'

He heads off towards the rise. The Doctor's long legs eat up the distance in no time and very soon you and Martha are chasing the Doctor's plimsolls up a rocky slope. But, just before the summit, he ducks down and motions you to do the same.

'What's over there?' asks Martha.

'Come and see — but carefully,' whispers the Doctor.

You crawl up to the edge of the ridge. The view takes your breath away. Here is a huge, sprawling mass of armoured cars and tanks. Exhaust fumes clog the air but you can see hundreds — perhaps thousands — of robots marching around among the vehicles. At the very edge of the nearest column of robots is a small concrete bunker.

> **The bunker could be important: if you suggest making for the bunker, go to 94. You are worried there are too many robots here: if you think you should retreat, go to 14.**

84 You hurry to catch up with the Doctor. 'I can hear something up ahead,' you tell him.

He stops and listens. You can all hear the sound of heavy machinery and the deep, aggressive snarl of military engines. 'You're right — sounds big, too.'

'Whatever it is, it's just over that rise,' says Martha, pointing to a craggy slope directly ahead. 'We'd better take a look.'

Carefully, you make your way to the top of the rise, and, keeping low, peer down at a scene of massive military activity. There is a huge, sprawling mass of armoured cars and tanks. Exhaust fumes clog the air but you can see hundreds — perhaps thousands — of robots marching around among the vehicles. But at the very edge of the nearest column of robots you spot a small concrete bunker.

The Doctor's examining the entrance to the bunker through a pair of folding opera glasses he has produced from one of his suit pockets. 'I think we should take a closer look at that,' he murmurs.

Go to 94.

85 The smoke of battle is still thick; in the poor visibility you may stand a chance of making a run for it. You sprint away into the fog. Lasers zip through the air after you, but they're wide of the mark. You hear the sound of a large robot machine ahead and veer away, beginning to choke on the dust and smoke. You have to stop running soon and think what to do. You're completely lost. There's now no sign of the Doctor or Martha or even the TARDIS, and you can still hear the mechanical grind of giant caterpillar tracks crunching over the battlefield nearby. You force yourself to move on, heading in the opposite direction.

Soon you can make out a small bunker in the distance. It looks unguarded.

If you make for the bunker, go to 95. If you decide to continue searching for the Doctor and Martha, go to 15.

With a heavy sigh you step out from behind the police box, hands up.

But no one is looking at you. A battered hovercraft has hummed up to where the robots are holding the Doctor and Martha at gunpoint. It is piloted by another robot, which gestures for your friends to climb on. As the hovercraft turns to leave in a cloud of dust, you see Martha looking out of one of the windows at you. She gives you a sad wave.

You feel as though this is all going wrong. But at least you are free — or so you think. Suddenly a cold metal hand clamps down on your shoulder and you are lifted bodily into the air. A pair of green eyes stares at you from a rusted face. 'YOU CANNOT ESCAPE,' the robot tells you flatly, and throws you to the floor of the truck with such force that you lose consciousness.

When you wake up the truck is still rumbling over the battlefield. You rest against the TARDIS for a while as the truck continues to crawl over the ragged countryside. All you can see is war-torn desert and the wreckage of destroyed robots and aircraft. Black smoke drifts across the desert.

'Where are we going?' you ask, addressing the immobile robot sharing the vehicle with you.

'BUNKER G87,' the robot intones. It turns its baleful gaze in your direction. 'WHERE YOU WILL BE ANALYSED AND THEN

ELIMINATED.'

There's not much else to say. After a while the truck grinds to a stop and you are ordered out. There is a small bunker in front of you.

'ENTER THE BUNKER,' the robot instructs, prodding you with its gun.

Go to 95.

'**W**elcome to the Eye,' says the robot. Its voice is smooth and calm. It waves a slender mechanical hand at the glass tube, which immediately slides open with a soft hum.

The Doctor steps out with a grin. 'Hello! I'm the Doctor, this is Martha, and this is...'

'I know who you are,' interrupts the robot, gliding forward. 'I have been monitoring your progress ever since you arrived on Titanius.'

The Doctor frowns. 'Have you indeed?'

'I am Kelzo 472,' the robot continues. 'It is my duty to monitor the long battle below.'

'Below?' echoes Martha. 'Where are we exactly?'

'You are on a satellite in orbit around Titanius.'

The Doctor taps the glass tube and smiles. 'Really? Nice teleport, by the way...'

Go to 70.

The flyer suddenly goes into a steep dive. You lurch forward, both of you grabbing for the controls. The engine screams. You and Martha scream.

And then, amazingly, the flyer begins to level.

'We've done it!' shrieks Martha with delight.

You shake your head. 'No way — that wasn't us. Look!'

Martha looks up to where you're pointing and gasps. High above, hanging in the sky, is the largest aircraft you've ever seen — a massive sky station, covered in hundreds of portholes, landing strips and helipads. Huge engines keep the edifice aloft, and hundreds of flyers and jet aircraft buzz around it like flies.

'Somehow that thing's caught us!'

'Tractor beam or something, I suppose,' agrees Martha.

Gradually, your flyer is dragged closer and closer to the monstrous vessel.

Go to 2.

Grant Kimer is the leader of a group of men and women struggling to stay alive on the planet. 'The robots are doing everything they can to wipe us out,' he explains.

'Why?' asks the Doctor.

'It's in their programming.'

Martha looks horrified. 'You mean they can't help it?'

'You could put it like that, I suppose,' shrugs Kimer. 'All I know is that they won't stop until we're all dead.'

'What happened?'

'When we came to this planet it was beautiful. We swore that we would never fight each other again — that we would always live in harmony and settle our differences peacefully.'

'Easier said than done,' the Doctor comments ruefully.

'We created the robots to fight each other. Disputes were settled that way — the robots fought, nobody got hurt.'

'Let me guess,' the Doctor says, 'the robots got carried away?'

'We lost control. They couldn't stop fighting. Eventually they started to repair themselves, improve themselves, build completely new robots to help them. It just got out of hand. We couldn't stop them.'

'And now they've turned on you as well as each other,' Martha realises. 'That's awful.'

'They've driven us underground like rats,' Kimer says. 'We're barely surviving — there aren't many of us left.'

Go to 97.

The machine-beast stares balefully at you. You feel yourself trembling with fear — it's so powerful, so alien, and the smell of engine oil is overpowering.

'ALL HUMANS MUST BE REMOVED FROM THE PLANET!' booms the voice.

'Wait!' shouts the Doctor. He frowns. 'Removed?'

'It means killed, Doctor,' says Grant Kimer. 'That's all they do — kill us and each other.'

'Can't we discuss this first?' the Doctor asks the giant metal creature.

'ALL HUMANS MUST BE REMOVED FROM THE PLANET!'

'I take it the answer is *no*...'

Suddenly the mechanical arms lash out and encircle you, the Doctor, Martha and Kimer in a crushing grip...

If you think the beast is going to kill you, go to 100. If you should wait and see what it wants, go to 72.

'There'll be a robot on guard outside,' you point out.

'I know,' says the Doctor. 'That's why we're going out the back door.'

He runs the screwdriver over the rear wall and a hatch slides open. 'There's always an emergency access hatch in these things. Come on!'

You clamber through the hatch and find yourself in a narrow metal tunnel just wide enough for you to crawl down.

'Budge up!' says Martha as she climbs in behind you. 'What's this — a ventilation shaft or something?'

'Something,' the Doctor's voice echoes back. 'Robots don't have any need for ventilation!'

You reach a junction in the shaft.

'Left or right?' asks the Doctor.

If you go left, turn to 30. If you go right, turn to 52.

'Let me try,' you say, grabbing the controls. You wrench the handlebars back as far as you can go, and, engines protesting with a terrible shriek, the flyer pulls out of its dive.

'Oh, well done!' yells the Doctor delightedly. 'I really like you!'

Before you have time to smile back, Martha taps you on the shoulder. She's pointing at something in the sky above you.

It's an enormous aircraft, the size of a building, held aloft by immense antigravity generators. The three of you stare at it in awe. The sky station's engines are deafening. You all cover your ears as the flyer is sucked into one of the tractor chutes beneath the craft like grit into a vacuum cleaner. There are robot guards waiting for you. They drag you off the flyer and march you through several gloomy corridors until they reach a heavy metal doorway. The robot opens the door and orders you through into another passageway.

'What is this place?' asks the Doctor.

'THIS IS MACHINA 1,' the robot tells you.

'Thanks,' replies the Doctor. 'And goodbye.'

He aims his sonic screwdriver at the door control and it hums shut — separating you from the robot.

'Come on!' the Doctor yells, grabbing hold of you and Martha. 'Run!'

Go to 52.

93 | '**W**AIT!' rasps the robot, moving towards the Doctor.

But it's too late. The sonic screwdriver whirrs and the teleport controls operate.

You feel a sudden, strange sensation — almost as if you're moving, or falling, and the bunker simply disappears from view… to be replaced by an entirely different environment.

The grim concrete has gone. In its place are steel and white plastic — all brilliantly lit. The Doctor, Martha and you are standing in some sort of sterile glass tube about three metres in diameter.

On the other side of the glass a strange figure is watching you. It's another robot — but this one is clean, elegant, with shining chrome skin and a single green eye.

'Ah,' says the Doctor. 'Now that I wasn't expecting.'

Go to 87.

'That bunker must be guarded for a reason,' you point out.

There are two vicious-looking robot dogs standing by the entrance.

The Doctor nods. 'Come on — now's our chance!'

The last phalanx of robots has trooped past leaving a cloud of dust hanging in the air. Hidden from view, the three of you scramble down the slope and run for the bunker.

'They won't hear us over all the stomping around,' notes the Doctor. 'But we'll have to distract those robot dogs somehow.'

'Here,' you say, picking up a handful of gravel and flinging it at a nearby tank. The stones rattle loudly against its metal flank and the dogs immediately move to investigate.

Quickly the Doctor opens the bunker door with the sonic screwdriver.

If you go in first, turn to 95. If you follow the Doctor and Martha inside, go to 102.

You step inside the bunker. The door immediately clangs shut behind you and you are completely alone. You twist around and bang on the rusty armour plate but it's useless. No one can hear you. You're trapped.

Slowly the bunker fills with light, revealing a small, circular chamber with a raised platform at its centre. There's a control pad on a stand next to the platform. A brief inspection shows it to be a matter transmitter. Some people call it a teleport.

The controls look complex. You spend a minute or two studying them. It's obvious that the only way out of here is via the teleport — but dare you risk it? It could lead anywhere — back outside, to another bunker, or even somewhere off the planet. You would be completely separated from the Doctor and Martha.

But the bunker door is locked. There's no other way out. You don't really have a choice.

Go to 104.

Gripping the gun hard, you move along the trench. You don't know if you could actually fire it — but neither will anyone else.

Slowly you creep forward into the smoke.

'What are you waving that thing around for?' says a familiar voice. It's the Doctor, and Martha's with him. What a relief! But the Doctor's staring at your robot gun disapprovingly.

'I thought you might be robots or something,' you say.

'Best get rid of it,' Martha advises. 'There's more than enough guns being used on this planet as it is.'

'Exactly what I thought,' says the Doctor.

Go to 73.

'There must be some way of stopping them,' you say.

Kimer nods. 'There is. These components are all part of a robot's central computer control system — its brain, if you like. Perhaps we can use the signals it transmits back to base to locate the main robot HQ and launch an attack.'

'Sounds feasible,' says the Doctor. 'Let's have a look at it.'

He pops on his spectacles and takes a look at the electronic equipment. He fiddles with some of the circuits and then smiles. 'Oh, yes. I think we're in luck! There's still some of the memory core left, by the looks of it. We should be able to — '

At that moment the tunnel suddenly caves in with an enormous crash. Masonry and dust fly everywhere, and you glimpse several metallic creatures dropping down into the chamber — robot dogs! Mechanical growls fill the air. Green eyes glow fiercely in the gloom, looking all around for targets.

If you turn and run, go to 106. If you try to find the Doctor and Martha, go to 114.

'Run for it!' you yell, sprinting past the nearest robot and dodging between another two. You are aware of the Doctor and Martha making a break for it as well — in different directions, probably to confuse the robots and draw their fire.

But these robots mean business, and their weapons are lethal: you watch in horror as one of them shoots the fallen girl at point-blank range.

Another robot's gun discharges and the earth explodes in front of you. You can hear the robots barking orders and more gunfire.

Suddenly the ground opens up beneath you — you've run straight into another crater. You tumble down in a cloud of dust and skid to a halt.

Immediately you jump to your feet. You may have to run again.

Someone — or something — is approaching you through the dust.

If you think it's the Doctor or Martha, go to 65. If you think it's another robot, go to 66.

Inside the rucksack is a robot's head. There are patches of rust on the metal and oily wires hanging from the neck.

'Someone's lost their head,' the Doctor says drily.

'It's what's inside that matters,' says Tela. She sounds very weak. Her wounds are taking their final toll.

The Doctor is already peering into the metal skull. 'Couldn't agree with you more — but what is inside, apart from a basic robot computer brain?'

'Take out the primary communications coil,' instructs Tela, her voice barely above a whisper. She's fading fast. 'Whatever happens, you must... get it to... Grant Kimer.'

'Grant Kimer,' Martha repeats. 'Where will we find him?'

But Tela is dead. Carefully, gently, Martha closes the girl's eyes.

Go to 6.

'It's going to kill us!' you wail as the tentacle lifts you into the air and squeezes tighter.

The Doctor is looking at the creature in wonder. 'The Omnipus!' he gasps.

Then the machine-beast suddenly lowers itself into the ground, submerging beneath the earth. For a moment everything goes dark and you think you might suffocate.

Then you find yourself in an enormous subterranean cavern. The Omnipus fills the space — thousands of metal tentacles slither and coil with a screech of metal on metal. The burning green eye illuminates the cave with a ghastly glow.

The tentacles have brought your friends as well.

'I take it we're in the lair of Titanius?' asks the Doctor.

'I AM TITANIUS!' booms the creature. 'ALL HUMANS WILL BE REMOVED — '

'Yes, yes, you've told us already. Is that what this war is all about?'

'WAR? I AM NOT PROGRAMMED FOR WAR. THIS CANNOT BE CORRECT!'

'Your robots have practically wiped out humankind on this planet. Now they've turned on each other. It's terrible up there, you know.'

There is a pause. 'I CANNOT HALT THE ROBOTS. I HAVE A FAULT IN MY PROGRAMMING.'

'You mean you're not feeling very well,' the Doctor says. 'Poor Omnipus!'

'What you need is a Doctor,' grins Martha.

Go to 74.

'Martha's right,' you say firmly. 'Going back would be suicide — we'd be throwing our lives away for nothing.'

The Doctor considers. 'Kimer's got the robot brain components. They could be vital!'

'Maybe we could split up?' suggests Martha.

Before you can protest, a shadow falls over the rocks and the three of you look up to see a huge robot glaring down at you. A heavy blaster mounted on its shoulder swivels around to point directly at you.

'It's traditional to raise your hands at this juncture,' says the Doctor.

It's just one robot. If you want to make a break for it, go to 53. If you think you'd better surrender — for now — go to 110.

102 | **Q**uickly the three of you slip inside and the Doctor locks the door behind you.

It's dark. Martha finds her key ring torch and shines the light directly in front of you.

There's a robot dog standing guard. Its eyes begin to glow as it sees you, and a low mechanical growl echoes round the chamber.

'Uh-oh,' says Martha.

'This isn't a bunker,' you say. 'It's a kennel!'

The dog begins to move towards you. You can hear its metal joints squeaking and the sound of its motors grinding.

If you think you should go back outside, go to 73. If you think you should stay where you are, go to 71.

103 The Doctor has it open in a moment and the three of you find yourselves in a huge underground cavern. It has been carved out of solid rock, but reinforced with massive steel buttresses and lined with bank after bank of computers and control systems. Lights flash and machinery hums.

'Look!' you shout, pointing to a familiar blue police box parked in one corner.

'It's the TARDIS!' laughs Martha. 'The robots must've brought it here — but why?'

'YOU ARE FORBIDDEN TO ENTER THIS CHAMBER,' booms a voice from all around you. The lights on the computer bank pulse in time with the words.

The Doctor folds his arms. 'I assume you're the one responsible for all this?'

'THIS IS OPERATIONS CONTROL,' the voice replies.

'Very grand,' remarks the Doctor. 'I suppose the robots are all controlled from here, then?'

'I AM IN DIRECT CONTACT WITH EVERY COMBATANT.'

'Oh, even better! This is gonna be easier than I thought!'

'WHAT DO YOU MEAN?'

'Well, in order to stop all those robots tearing lumps out of each other and the planet for absolutely no reason at all, all I have to do… is stop you.'

Go to 28.

---

104 You operate the teleport controls and feel yourself immediately fading away.

When you materialise, you are standing in a plastic tube that rises into the ceiling. You walk out into a sterile, white environment completely unlike anything you've seen on the robot planet.

The teleport buzzes again behind you and to your astonishment the Doctor and Martha appear.

'Hello!' The Doctor looks as if he's just stepped off a bus. 'Good to see you again — is this the main control centre?'

A large glass tube drops down, trapping you all inside. A door slides open in the wall and a gleaming white robot glides forward, fixing you with one eye…

Go to 87.

'We all stick together,' says the Doctor firmly. Even standing with his hands on his head at gunpoint, he can exert his authority.

The bunker door grinds open, flakes of rust falling away from the thick armour plate. Inside is a flight of concrete steps leading down to an underground chamber full of strange electronic equipment.

The Doctor's immediately intrigued. 'This looks like the controls for a teleport relay,' he says, examining one of the consoles.

'Teleport?' you echo. 'Where to?'

'Good question!' The Doctor whirls to face the nearest robot. 'Got a good answer?'

'THE TRANSMAT IS LINKED TO OPERATIONAL HEADQUARTERS.'

'Well,' the Doctor says with a smile, 'what are we waiting for?'

Go to 111.

106 The narrow tunnel is suddenly invaded by robot dogs — bulky, rusting beasts with angry green eyes and jaws like steel traps. Heavy pistons and hydraulic cables power the hounds' legs as they leap on to the soldiers. The tunnel reverberates with the sound of weapons firing and mechanical snarls.

Panicking, you turn and run, splashing through the water that swills around the tunnel floor. You can't see the Doctor or Martha anywhere, but if you wait around here you're going to get eaten!

Stumbling down a passage, you find an old metal ladder set into the side. It leads up to another manhole cover. Hurriedly you mount the ladder and try to open the hatch. It's very stiff. You can hear the yells of the soldiers and the crunch of steel teeth on bone behind you.

If you think you should stop and go back to help, go to 114. If you think should try the hatch again and get out, go to 80.

Together, you and Martha help the Doctor to his feet. The sky station tilts dramatically, nearly tipping you all over.

'The whole station's going down,' realises Martha. 'It's the end of the robot war — and the end of us!'

'Need to find a flyer,' says the Doctor. 'The robots are all out of order, but the flyers will still work.'

The station is listing heavily. After a few minutes it starts to fall. But you manage to find a bay containing a number of flyers ready for action. Climbing past the motionless robots, you help the Doctor and Martha on to a flyer and take the controls. The flyer slips free of the station just as the entire edifice plummets towards the ground.

The explosion when it hits is enormous, and can be seen from hundreds of miles away. The flyer is buffeted by the shockwave, but you are able to control it. A little later, you bring it safely to a halt by a familiar blue police box.

'That was a bit too close,' comments Martha. 'What'll happen now?'

'Can't we let the nearby worlds know that this planet is safe now?' you ask.

'Good idea,' nods the Doctor. 'Don't want to let it all rust away, do we?" The Doctor tosses you the TARDIS key. 'Go on,' he urges. 'You've earned it.'

Smiling happily, you unlock the police box doors, and the three of you go inside — on your way to yet more adventures.

THE END

'This can't go on,' you say. 'It's stupid and pointless and it's ruining the planet.'

'Can you stop the robots fighting, Kelzo?' asks Martha.

The robot seems to consider the question carefully. 'I could send a command to cease fire through the communications network which links all the robots, yes,' he says. 'But I have not been programmed to do so. I have only been programmed to monitor the conflict.'

'Oh, we can soon alter that,' says the Doctor, taking out his sonic screwdriver and raising an eyebrow.

Kelzo is not a battle robot and does not offer any resistance. It takes the Doctor less than ten minutes to reprogram him — ten minutes well spent. Kelzo seems almost relieved when the Doctor closes the inspection hatch on his head.

'At last,' says the robot quietly. 'The long task can be finished.'

He works at the control console for a few seconds. 'There — the ceasefire signal has been sent. The robots will fight no more. My job is done.'

The Doctor scratches his ear. 'I've a feeling it's only just beginning...'

Go to 39.

109 A little while later, you are all standing by the TARDIS. The Doctor is shaking hands with Grant Kimer, and some of the other humans are chatting to Martha.

'We can't thank you enough, Doctor,' Kimer is saying. 'Every single robot and machine on the planet is defunct. It's a miracle!'

'Not quite,' the Doctor smiles. 'It's actually a macro-kinetic sonic impulse on a feedback loop through the communications network. But it'll still do the trick. The planet is yours again.'

Kimer laughs. 'All I know is that for the first time in decades we can't hear the sound of gunfire, thanks to you.'

'I couldn't have done it without my friends,' The Doctor puts his arms around you and Martha. 'Speaking of which, they both have appointments on the other side of the galaxy — so if you don't mind, we'll be off…'

Before Kimer can protest, the three of you enter the TARDIS. A moment later it vanishes, no doubt on its way to further adventures!

THE END

Carefully, you raise your hands.

The robot looks at you without a trace of emotion. It is nothing more than a machine following instructions – a program – and that may be your best hope.

'I know what you're thinking,' mutters the Doctor, seeing the look in your eyes. 'Something is controlling them – and if we can get at that something, maybe we can stop them.'

'STOP TALKING,' the robot orders.

'You need to take us back to your base,' the Doctor tells it. 'I have important information for your controller.'

'WHAT INFORMATION?'

'I can only tell your controller.'

'TELL ME.'

'I can't,' the Doctor risks a slight smile. 'It's against my programming.'

The robot whirrs and clicks as it considers. Then it reaches out and grabs you...

Go to 72.

111 'ANALYSIS,' declares the robot, and suddenly the three of you are enveloped by a crackling energy field. You can't move a muscle.

A robot steps forward and stands directly in front of you. Its green eyes glow ever more fiercely until your vision is filled by an emerald light and the robot's relentless gaze penetrates your every thought and memory.

Eventually the blinding glare diminishes. When you finally regain your senses, you see that the Doctor and Martha have both undergone a similar interrogation.

'YOU TWO ARE HUMAN,' says the robot, indicating you and Martha. 'YOU WILL BE ELIMINATED.'

'Wrong!' yells the Doctor, and the robot turns to see him holding his sonic screwdriver against the teleport control panel.

If you think the Doctor's about to operate the teleport, go to 93. If you think the Doctor's going to wreck the control panel, go to 33.

112 There's no more time for talk. You all feel a faint trembling in the ground beneath your feet — and then, suddenly it erupts.

Mechanical arms — segmented tentacles — burst out of the soil all around you. The earth cracks open and a gigantic robotic creature starts to emerge. Its tentacles flail madly, grabbing soldiers and throwing them around like dolls. At the centre of the machine is a single, massive glowing eye. It swivels and focuses with a motorised whine on you and your friends.

'HUMANS!' screeches a loud, ugly voice from beneath the ground. You crawl over to the Doctor and Martha. The Doctor is looking grimly at the machine-creature.

'What do you want from us?' yells the Doctor.

'ALL HUMANS MUST DIE!'

Go to 90.

113 'Now you're talking,' says the Doctor with a huge grin. 'There's music, and theatre, and books and...'

Martha laughs as the Doctor rambles. 'And ice cream!' she adds gleefully. 'And dancing!'

Caught up in the mood, you add a few of your own favourite things. Even the injured Grant Kimer is smiling. Seeing his chance, the Doctor gets to work on the robot, still chatting away.

'So there's a lot more than war. In fact, war should take up the tiniest part of your programming. We all need to fight for something, when we have to — but not just because we can't think of anything else to do!'

He finishes his work with the sonic screwdriver and snaps shut the access lid on the computer. 'That should do it. Brand new program — and it's being downloaded to every other robot too. It'll be a brand new start. Rebuild the planet, make peace with Grant Kimer and the rest of the humans left here.'

'We're tired of fighting, too,' Kimer sighs. 'It's time we made peace.'

'THE WAR OF THE ROBOTS IS OVER AT LAST, DOCTOR — THANKS TO YOU,' says the robot. 'WHAT CAN WE DO FOR YOU IN RETURN?'

'Well,' the Doctor replies, putting his arms around you and Martha. 'We wouldn't say no to a lift back to the TARDIS.'

THE END

---

114 You rush back to help — but it's panic in the tunnel. All you can see are men running and the robot dogs attacking in a mechanical frenzy.

'This way!' says the Doctor suddenly, grabbing you by the scruff of the neck and hauling you upwards. He's leaning down from another access ladder. Martha is just above him, opening a manhole.

'Use this!' shouts the Doctor, thrusting something into your hand.

It's the sonic screwdriver. You aim it down the tunnel and an ear-splitting squeal makes the robot dogs suddenly start chasing their tails.

'Ultrasonics,' grins the Doctor. 'Always works on dogs!'

Go to 76.

115 'Grab the controls!' you yell as the flyer suddenly dives.

Martha leans forward and pulls the flyer's joystick back. She manages to pull the flyer level but the engine's howling. There's smoke pouring from the back of the vehicle and you know you don't have much longer left. It's too far down now — if you lose power you'll crash.

'I think we're done for,' Martha says.

If you think the flyer's going to crash, go to 88. If you think there's a chance you can regain control, go to 58.

---

116 But lying low isn't going to do you any good at all. Almost immediately, you feel the ground beneath you beginning to shake, and something huge and metal thrusts its way out of the crumbling soil. It's a giant, robotic machine — you glimpse any number of mechanical arms flailing around as the strange creature emerges from the earth... and then you realise something awful.

Clutched in its steel grippers are the Doctor, Martha and Grant Kimer. The machine has hauled them up through the ground. Coughing and spluttering, the Doctor waves a greeting.

'Nice to see you again so soon,' he declares.

Go to 90.

'Run for it!' you yell, sprinting past the nearest robot and dodging between another two. Dimly you are aware of the Doctor and Martha making a break for it as well — in different directions, probably to confuse the robots and draw their fire.

But these robots mean business, and their weapons are lethal: a gun discharges and the earth explodes in front of you. You can hear the robots barking orders and more gunfire.

Suddenly the ground opens up beneath you — you've run straight into another crater. You tumble down in a cloud of dust and skid to a halt.

Immediately you jump to your feet. You may have to run again.

Someone — or something — is approaching you through the dust.

If you think it's the Doctor or Martha, go to 65. If you think it's another robot, go to 66.

Step into a world of wonder and
mystery with Sarah Jane and
her gang in:

1. Invasion of the Bane
2. Revenge of the Slitheen
3. Eye of the Gorgon
4. Warriors of the Kudlak

And don't miss these other exciting
adventures with the Doctor!

1. The Spaceship Graveyard
2. Alien Arena
3. The Time Crocodile
4. The Corinthian Project
5. The Crystal Snare
6. War of the Robots
7. Dark Planet
8. The Haunted Wagon Train